MEET ALL THESE FRIENDS IN BUZZ BOOKS:

Thomas the Tank Engine
Fireman Sam
Bugs Bunny
Toucan 'Tecs
Barney
Tugs
Police Academy
Gremlins
Micro Machines

First published 1991 by Buzz Books,
an imprint of Reed International Books Ltd
Michelin House, 81 Fulham Road, London SW3 6RB

LONDON MELBOURNE AUCKLAND

Flintstones copyright © 1991 Hanna-Barbera Productions, Inc.
This edition copyright © 1991 William Heinemann Ltd

Text adapted from an original cartoon entitled
Swimming Pool Story

ISBN 1 85591 160 4

Printed and bound in the UK by BPCC Hazell Books Ltd

THE FLINTSTONES™

IN

SWIMMING POOL PRANKS

Story adapted by Helen Lloyd
from an original cartoon

Illustrations by CLIC!

buzz books

Barney and Fred had had an argument.
They still weren't speaking, so Barney
decided to collect some things Fred had
borrowed from him.

"Oh and er, I need the ladder too,
Wilma," said Barney.

"Fine," said Wilma. "Help yourself."

Unfortunately, Fred was still using the ladder!

"Why you . . ." said Fred, giving chase into Barney's garden.

"Hey, what's going on?" he yelled as he fell into an enormous hole. "What are you doing Barney? What's the crater for?"

"I'm building a swimming pool, Fred,"
said Barney.

"Is that so?" said Fred, suddenly
interested. "What would you say to the
kind offer of a free extra half to your pool?
That way, you get a pool twice as big!"

"How do you mean, Fred?" asked
Barney.

"I mean, old pal and esteemed neighbour, that if I have half the pool in my garden you'll have a bigger pool for the same money – right?"

"Er, right, Fred," said Barney.

"Good thinking, Barney!"

So, poor Barney dug the whole pool –
including Fred's half.

"Now, all it needs is filling, Barney boy.
4000 buckets should do it. I'll give you a
hand with the first one just to show you
what a big hearted guy I am!"

"Can't stop, Barney – time to get a few new swimming togs. See you later. Just think Barney – barbecues, swimming parties – it's going to be great!"

"Just think," said Barney wearily, as he trudged up and down.

11

When Fred drew up outside the cave later,
Barney called out: "Hey Fred! This is the
last bucket!"

"Oh boy, oh boy, I'll race you in, Barney!
Yabba dabba doo!"

When Fred and Barney dived in, they
missed the pool – but not each other!

SOMETHING TELLS
ME THIS POOL IS
GOING TO CAUSE
PROBLEMS!

Later, Fred was relaxing in the pool on his
airbed. "Oh honey," he called, "do you
think you can bring my lunch out here?
I'm just so comfortable!"

"Oh all right, Fred," sighed Wilma.

14

"Aaahhh! What's that?" she shrieked.

"What do you think of my spear fishing outfit, Wilma?" giggled Barney.

"Terrific, Barney – you'll scare the fish to death," said Wilma.

The pool was a big hit – especially with Barney's friends. Almost every day, Fred came home looking forward to a long cool swim, only to find the pool full.

"Who is it today, Barney?" asked Fred sarcastically.

"The YCMA, Fred – Young Cavemen's
Association. They're having a great time!"

"That's it!" said Fred, stomping off
towards his cave. "I'm not having my half
of the pool used by everyone in the
neighbourhood!"

Two hours later, Fred had put up a fence across the pool.

"Time to enjoy my half of the pool in peace," he said, and changed for a swim.

WHAT'S FRED UP TO NOW...

What he didn't know was that after the Young Cavemen's Association party broke up, Barney had drained his half of the water out of the pool, so Fred ended up in a nose dive!

18

Fred was relaxing indoors when he
overheard Betty and Wilma talking about
yet another party!

"I've had enough," muttered Fred.
"Time to stop this joking around with one
of my jokes!"

He picked up the phone and dialled.

"Is that you, Charlie?" he said.

"Hi, Fred," said Charlie. "How's things?"

Fred giggled as he explained what he wanted Charlie to do.

"That's fixed it for Barney and his party! Heh! Heh! Heh!" said Fred as he hung up the phone.

Lots of people arrived for the party, and
then there was a knock at Fred's front door.

When he opened it, Barney and Betty
stood there.

"What's the cake for?" growled Fred.

When they started singing, Fred didn't
know what to say.

"Surprise, surprise!" said Barney. "This party's for you!"

"Me? Why? I mean, that's real kind of you – play the drums Barney, and I'll take the strings – this is going to be some party!"

The party was a great success, but they didn't notice the music was getting louder and louder.

It got so noisy that an angry neighbour called the police.

When two police officers arrived a few moments later, Fred didn't worry.

"Charlie! Glad you could make it – and a friend too! No need for the disturbing the peace routine – just join in!"

"My name's not Charlie, and if you don't stop this party now, I'm going to run you in!"

"Oh, I get it – I'll go along with the gag, Charlie," .whispered Fred. "Right," he shouted, "just watch me run *you* in!"

Fred heard a small voice beside him.

"Hi, Fred."

"Oh, hi Charlie – Charlie!"

"I couldn't get the police suit – thought I'd come to the party anyway."

"This party's over," said the other police officer. "Get in the car, Mr Flintstone!"

"What a disaster!" moaned Fred as he sat in the police cell later. "I didn't even get a piece of my cake!"

"Psst, Fred," said Barney. "We'll get you out of here in a jiffy. In the meantime, here's something for you."

"You're one of the good ones Barney,"
sighed Fred.

"Just think of it this way, Fred," said
Barney. "You're going to miss loads of turns
at cleaning out the pool!"

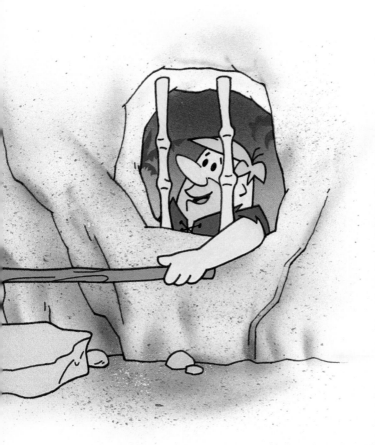